THERE'S NO PLACE LIKE
SCHOOL

CLASSROOM POEMS

SELECTED BY
JACK PRELUTSKY

ILLUSTRATIONS BY
JANE MANNING

Greenwillow Books, *An Imprint of* HarperCollins*Publishers*

There's No Place Like School: Classroom Poems. Text copyright © 2010 by Jack Prelutsky. Illustrations copyright © 2010 by Jane Manning. All rights reserved.
Manufactured in China. For information address HarperCollins Children's Books, a division of HarperCollins Publishers, 10 East 53rd Street, New York, NY 10022.
www.harpercollinschildrens.com. Watercolors were used to prepare the full-color art. The text type is Shannon.
Library of Congress Cataloging-in-Publication Data: There's no place like school : classroom poems / written and edited by Jack Prelutsky ; illustrated by Jane Manning.
p. cm. "Greenwillow Books." ISBN 978-0-06-082338-2 (trade bdg.) — ISBN 978-0-06-082339-9 (lib. bdg.) 1. Schools—Juvenile poetry. 2. Classrooms—Juvenile
poetry. 3. Children's poetry, American. I. Prelutsky, Jack. II. Manning, Jane, (date) ill. PS595.S34T47 2010   811'.60809282—dc22   2009020373

10 11 12 13 14 SCP 10 9 8 7 6 5 4 3 2 1   First Edition   Greenwillow Books

"Going to School" from *All the Day Long*, by Nina Payne (Atheneum Publishers, 1973). Copyright © 1973 by Nina Payne. Reprinted with the permission of the estate of Nina Payne.
"School Bus" copyright © by Lee Bennett Hopkins. First appeared in *School Supplies*, by Lee Bennett Hopkins, published by Simon & Schuster. Reprinted by permission of Curtis Brown, Ltd.
"Show and Tell" and "Cursive Writing" from *Somebody Catch My Homework* by David L. Harrison (Wordsong, an imprint of Boyds Mills Press, 1993). Reprinted with the permission of Boyds Mills
Press, Inc. Text copyright © 1993 by David L. Harrison.
"Not Fair" from *Did You See What I Saw?* by Kay Winters, copyright © 1996 by Kay Winters. Used by permission of Viking Penguin, A Division of Penguin Young Readers Group, A Member of
Penguin Group (USA) Inc., 345 Hudson Street, New York, NY 10014. All rights reserved.
 "Don't Ask Me" © 1990 by Yolanda Nave. By permission of Edite Kroll Literary Agency Inc.
"Countdown to Recess" from *The Goof Who Invented Homework and Other School Poems* by Kalli Dakos, copyright © 1996 by Kalli Dakos. Used by permission of Dial Books for Young Readers,
A Division of Penguin Young Readers Group, A Member of Penguin Group (USA) Inc., 345 Hudson Street, New York, NY 10014. All rights reserved.
 "The Drinking Fountain" and "When the Teacher Isn't Looking" © 2005 by Kenn Nesbitt. Reprinted from *When the Teacher Isn't Looking* with the permission of Meadowbrook Press.
"Why the Frog in Our Class Is Purple" reprinted with the permission of Simon & Schuster Books for Young Readers, an imprint of Simon & Schuster Children's Publishing Division, from *Put Your Eyes
Up Here and Other School Poems*, by Kalli Dakos. Text copyright © 2003 Kalli Dakos.
"Lunchroom Magic" from *A Fury of Motion: Poems for Boys* by Charles Ghigna (Wordsong, an imprint of Boyds Mills Press, 2003). Reprinted with the permission of Boyds Mills Press, Inc. Text
copyright © 2003 by Charles Ghigna.
"Grasshopper Gumbo" copyright © 1990 by Jack Prelutsky. Reprinted from *Something Big Has Been Here* (Greenwillow Books, 1990). Used by permission of HarperCollins Publishers.
"B-Ball" from *Almost Late to School and More School Poems* by Carol Diggory Shields, copyright © 2003 by Carol Diggory Shields. Used by permission of Dutton Children's Books,
A Division of Penguin Young Readers Group, A Member of Penguin Group (USA) Inc., 345 Hudson Street, New York, NY 10014. All rights reserved.
 "Classroom Globe" from *In the Spin of Things: Poetry of Motion* by Rebecca Kai Dotlich (Wordsong, an imprint of Boyds Mills Press, 2003). Reprinted with the permission of Boyds Mills Press, Inc.
Text copyright © 2003 by Rebecca Kai Dotlich.
"It's Today?" from *Nothing's the End of the World* by Sara Holbrook (Wordsong, an imprint of Boyds Mills Press, 1995). Reprinted with the permission of Boyds Mills Press, Inc. Text copyright © 1995
by Sara Holbrook.
"We're Shaking Maracas" copyright © 2006 by Jack Prelutsky. Reprinted from *What a Day It Was at School!* (Greenwillow Books, 2006). Used by permission of HarperCollins Publishers.
"Far Away" from *Lunch Money* by Carol Diggory Shields, copyright © 1995 by Carol Diggory Shields. Used by permission of Dutton Children's Books, A Division of Penguin Young Readers Group,
A Member of Penguin Group (USA) Inc., 345 Hudson Street, New York, NY 10014. All rights reserved.
"If Homework Were Banished" copyright © 2009 by Maura Lesse. Used by permission of the author, who controls all rights.

CONTENTS

Going to School

BY NINA PAYNE

Take the steps two at a time,
you're being chased by bears!
Dive into the river
at the bottom of the stairs!
Swim into the living room,
dry off on a stool,
put your coat on, button up
and race the bears to school!

School Bus

BY LEE BENNETT HOPKINS

This wide-awake
freshly-painted-yellow
school bus

readied for Fall

carries us all—

Sixteen boys—
Fourteen girls—
Thirty pairs of sleepy eyes

and
hundreds
upon
hundreds

of

school supplies.

Show-and-Tell

BY DAVID L. HARRISON

Billy brought his snake to school
For show-and-tell today.
"This snake belongs to me," he said.
"It's gentle as can be," he said.
"It wouldn't hurt a flea," he said.
But it swallowed him anyway.

Not Fair

By Kay Winters

Why is it true?
When I know the answer
wave my hand wildly
and leap from my seat
she calls on you.

How can it be?
When I haven't a clue
roll my eyes skyward
and slump in my chair
she calls on me.

Don't Ask Me

BY YOLANDA NAVE

Don't ask *me*
What's three plus three;
Oh please don't call my name.
Please don't say
We're going to play
Another numbers game.

What's ten minus four?
Four minus two?
I do apologize. . . .
But to be exact,
When I subtract
I get butterflies.

What's two from eleven?
One times seven?
I really cannot tell.
If you'll excuse me,
Numbers confuse me—
But I can spell very well.

Countdown to Recess

By Kalli Dakos

Sun climbs.
Wind chimes.
Five minutes until recess.

A baseball glove.
A game I love.
Four minutes until recess.

I whisper to Pat,
"Get ready to bat."
Three minutes until recess.

My work's all done.
I gotta run.
Two minutes until recess.

Clock, hurry!
Hands, scurry!
One minute until recess.

Brrrrrrrrrrrrrrrrrrrrrrrrrrrrrring!

Dash!
Gone in a flash!

The Drinking Fountain

By Kenn Nesbitt

The drinking fountain squirted me.
It shot right up my nose.
It felt as if I'd stuck my nostril
on the garden hose.

It squirted water in my eye
and also in my ear.
I'm having trouble seeing,
and it's awfully hard to hear.

The water squirted east and west.
It squirted north and south.
Upon my shirt, my pants, my hair—
but nothing in my mouth.

I'm sure that soon they'll fix it,
but until then, let me think . . .
Just whom can I convince that they
should come and have a drink?

Why the Frog in Our Class Is Purple

BY KALLI DAKOS

We were painting
A mural today,
The frog got loose,
What else can I say?

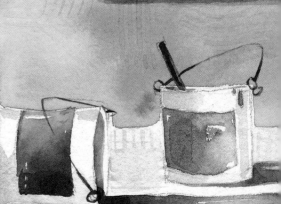

Cursive Writing

BY DAVID L. HARRISON

Who decides?
Who gets to choose?
Who dreams up these curlicues?
Should an 96 look like
A 9 and a 6?
Fiddlesticks!
Does a capital 2
That looks like a 2
Make sense to you?
Do I like these
Wiggles
And squiggles
And jiggles?
Hah!
What do I think
Of cursive writing?

Bah!

Lunchroom Magic

By Charles Ghigna

Of all the magic I have seen
My favorite, I suppose,
Was yesterday at lunch when Mark
Made milk come out his nose.

Grasshopper Gumbo

By Jack Prelutsky

SQUID SUCKER SUNDAES

FRIED FLYING FISH FINS

MEADOW MOUSE MORSELS

CRACKED CROCODILE CRUNCH

**The school cafeteria
serves them for lunch.**

B-Ball

BY CAROL DIGGORY SHIELDS

Rebound,
Swish sound.
Bounce, pass,
Break fast.
Three in the key,
Over to me.
Hook shot,
I'm hot.
Backcourt,
Shoot short.
Round the rim,
Almost in.
Free throw,
Way to go!
We won,
Had fun.

Classroom Globe

BY REBECCA KAI DOTLICH

Spinning, spinning,
round
and round,
a swirl of blue,
a whirl of brown;
mountain ranges,
oceans,
lakes,
islands,
foreign countries,
states.

Spinning, spinning,
stop!
Then linger.
Trace the earth
beneath
one finger.

Spinning, spinning,
round
and round,
a swirl of blue,
a whirl of brown.

Spinning, spinning,
round
and round.

It's Today?

BY SARA HOLBROOK

Frantic
panic,
sinking
sorrow.

The science test
is not
tomorrow.

When the Teacher Isn't Looking

BY KENN NESBITT

When the teacher's back is turned,
we never scream and shout.
Never do we drop our books
and try to freak her out.

No one throws a pencil
at the ceiling of the class.
No one tries to hit the fire alarm
and break the glass.

We don't cough in unison
and loudly clear our throats.
No one's shooting paper wads
or passing little notes.

She must think we're so polite.
We never make a peep.
Really, though, it's just because
we all go right to sleep.

We're Shaking Maracas

BY JACK PRELUTSKY

We're shaking maracas
And beating on drums,
We're tapping on tables
With fingers and thumbs.
We jingle our bells,
And we play tambourines,
We rattle our bottles
Of buttons and beans.

We're blowing our whistles
And tooting kazoos,
We're clanging our cymbals
As loud as we choose.
We stomp up and down
On the floor with our feet. . . .
We love making music,
The sound is so sweet.

Far Away

BY CAROL DIGGORY SHIELDS

Someone shouts in Annie's ear.

But what they're saying, she can't hear.

Buzzers buzz and school bells ring.

Annie doesn't hear a thing.

Friends can jostle, tug, and pinch.

Annie doesn't move an inch.

"Oooo, here comes a big black bug!"

Annie does not even shrug.

"Fire!" "Earthquake!" "Runaway bus!"

She remains oblivious

Until, at last, with a faraway look,

Annie smiles and shuts her book.

If Homework Were Banished

BY MAURA LESSE

If homework were banished, I'd probably never
Complain about anything, anything ever.
I doubt that I'd shed even one single tear
If I had no homework, not once in a year.

If homework were banished, my heart would be lighter,
My mood would stay sunny, my smile would be brighter,
I'd leap in the air and elatedly shout . . .

BUT

I've mountains of homework,
And see no way out.